This book belongs to

_____

This book is dedicated to children everywhere. You can make a difference.
Anthony and Alison

First Edition Published in 2010 by Joseph Publications
Text copyright © 2010 by Anthony Coccia
Illustration copyright © 2010 by Alison Lopez
All rights reserved. Published by Joseph Publications
Book design by Lauren Lopez

Library of Congress control number 2009907865

ISBN 13 digit 978-0-9773243-2-3
ISBN 10 digit 09773243-2-X

Printed on recycled paper.

Printed in China.
Midas Printing International Ltd.

The Turtle Story

Written by Anthony Coccia
Illustrated by Alison Lopez

Down in the swamp where the cattails grew,
Lived a family of turtles that everyone knew.
The swamp was once healthy, lively and green,
But people have littered and now it's unclean.
The turtles had to leave the swamp traveling alone,
For far away lands to find a new home.

Little boy turtle wanted to know,
"Now that we've left the swamp,
Where will we go?"
"To far away lands" father turtle replied,
"There's no litter there."
"It is a place where the water runs clean,
It will be the most beautiful place you've ever seen!"

The turtles moved on until they came to a stream.
It was the strangest stream they had ever seen.
The banks were all littered with old tin cans,
Candy wrappers, bottles and even frying pans!
Little boy turtle wanted to know,
"What's all this litter? And where should it go?"
"It's litter from people" mom turtle replied,
"As it belongs in a trash can" and dad turtle sighed.
"It's time for us to go, let's be on our way.
This stream is not clean, we cannot stay."

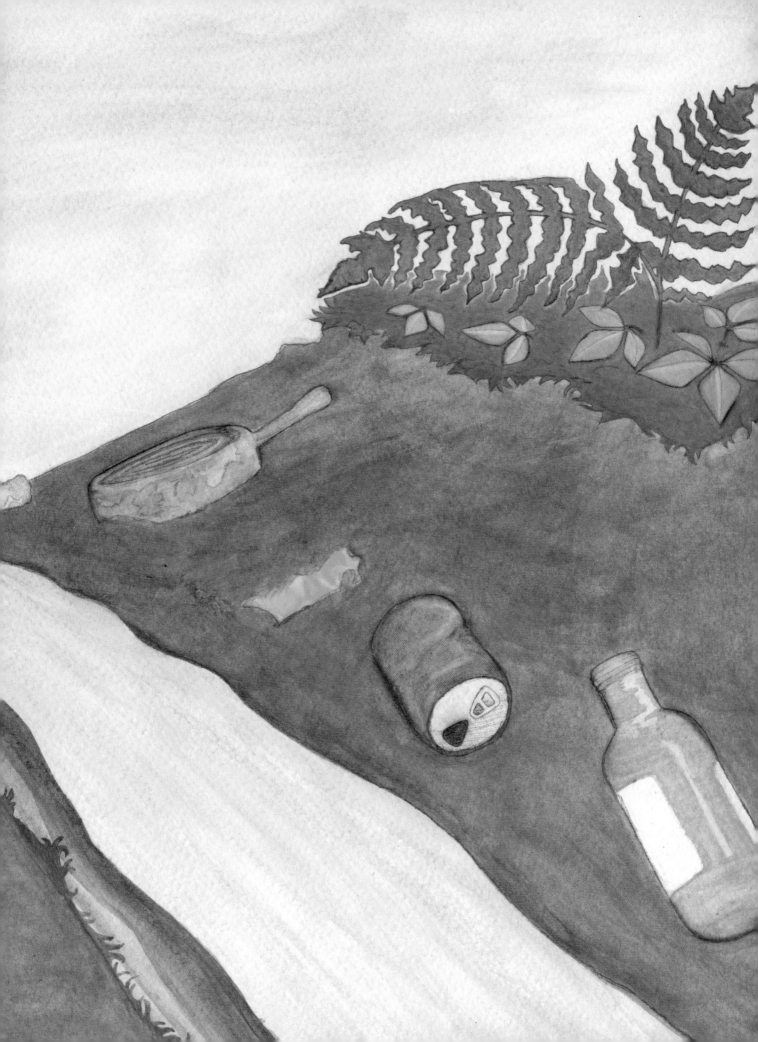

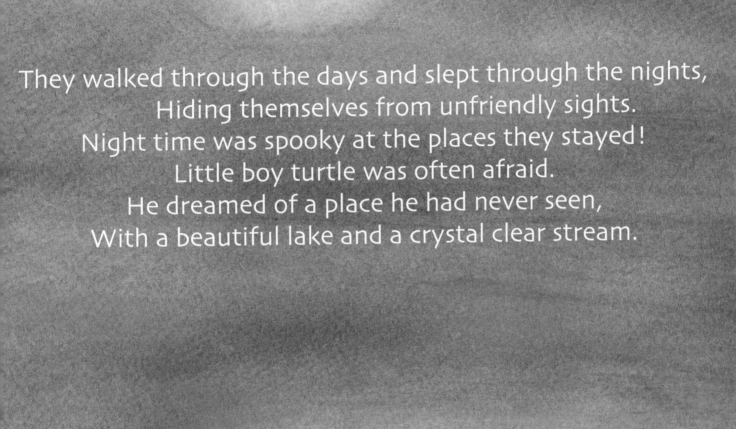

They walked through the days and slept through the nights,
Hiding themselves from unfriendly sights.
Night time was spooky at the places they stayed!
Little boy turtle was often afraid.
He dreamed of a place he had never seen,
With a beautiful lake and a crystal clear stream.

The turtles walked on, for many long hours,
Through the green grass and the wildflowers.
Over the rocks and under the trees,
Out of the sun and in the cool breeze.

They came to a pond with cut down logs,
And on these logs were very sad frogs.
Little boy turtle asked his dad,
"Why are these frogs all so sad?"

"They're sad said his dad because the trees have been cut."
"Too many trees lost and it's because of that,
That this place is no longer a habitat."
As the turtles moved on, tired and slow,
One frog said to the others, "It's time for us to go."

The turtles crossed paths with an old water snake,
He told them he just came down from the lake.
"I hope leaving for good, is not the only solution,
But it will be soon, if they don't clean the pollution."
The old water snake then slithered alone,
Toward the far away lands, to find his new home.

Turtles are small and turtles are slow,
But turtles are wise and they know where to go.
After the turtles stopped for a rest,
They picked the direction that would be the best.
On they walked through the wide open space,
Searching for comfort in a clean and safe place.

They came to a river at the end of the day,
Little boy turtle hoped they could stay.
As the sun began setting out in the sky,
An old rubber tire went floating right by!
"Can we stay here?" little boy turtle wanted to know.
"Not until its clean" said mother turtle,
And they continued to go.

Little boy turtle stopped on the trail,
He pulled in his head and he pulled in his tail.
"These places have litter and I don't know why."
Mother turtle was quick to reply,
"This journey is longer than we have expected,
Because the places we've seen have not been respected."
"When people litter they have a choice to make,
If people leave all of their litter behind,
A safe and clean home becomes harder to find."
Just at that moment the sun came through,
Lighting a spot with a wide open view.

They walked to the spot and stood in the light,
Right there before them was a breathtaking sight!
It was a lake unlike any they'd seen,
The lake was beautiful; the lake was clean.
There were no tires or tin cans,
No candy wrappers or frying pans.
There were healthy plants, fish and frogs,
Beavers, ducks and pollywogs.

The family of turtles found a new home,
To live and thrive and no longer roam
So remember,
The turtle's new home will remain litter free,
With a little help from you and from me!